The Giant Boy's Storybook Written Because Boys Are Superheroes

Inspiring Boy's Tales For Little Adventurers with Amazing Life Lessons

JOHN WASTON

ISBN - 9798807649256

This book belongs to

....

....

Contents

★ 6 ★

The Gribble

Just outside the woods, a boy called Jonah lived in a big old house with his dad and Grandpa Joe.

On most days, Jonah went to school in the village, his dad went to work at an office in the city, and Grandpa Joe looked after the chickens and goats until school was done.

When the school bell rang, Grandpa Joe would always be waiting to pick him up. They would walk home from school through the woods.

Jonah would tell his grandpa about his day, and Grandpa Joe would tell stories. Jonah's favourite stories were ones about monsters. Grandpa Joe told him all about the good and bad monsters that lived in the woods by their house.

On weekends, Jonah, his dad, and Grandpa Joe would do fun things together, like going to the park or the museum.

One day, Jonah's dad met a new friend named Cindy. Cindy had twins, a little girl and a little boy called Louise and Harold. Harold and Louise were two years younger than Jonah.

Jonah had fun when they all went out together, but still liked it best when it was just him, his dad, and Grandpa Joe.

On a sunny day one year after they met, Cindy and Jonah's dad got married. Cindy and the twins moved into the house in the woods and Jonah had to share his dad and Grandpa Joe every day.

Jonah didn't mind too much at first. But it wasn't long before Harold and Louise started getting on Jonah's nerves.

At home, Harold and Louise would go into Jonah's room without asking. They would play with his toys and mess up his things. Because they were little, they rarely got into trouble.

When Harold and Louise started going to Jonah's school, they followed Jonah around every recess. Even worse, they would try to join in games that they were too small to play. This made Jonah mad.

Every day after school, all four of them walked home through the woods. Grandpa Joe wouldn't tell monster stories anymore because the twins might get too scared. Jonah felt like he never had time alone with Grandpa Joe anymore.

One day, Jonah got so mad that he went to his room and closed the door. He leaned his back against it so the twins couldn't get inside and cried.

Jonah didn't come out of his room all night, not even for dinner. Before bedtime, Grandpa Joe knocked on his door.

When he asked Jonah what was wrong, Jonah said he was tired of the twins taking everything without asking. He told Grandpa Joe he missed spending time alone with just the three of them. He especially missed hearing monster stories.

Grandpa Joe listened patiently. Jonah told him all his bad feelings. He felt better after but was still sad. Grandpa Joe told him he understood that having a new little brother and sister was frustrating.

Grandpa Joe said that they should plan a fun activity together, a campout in the woods outside the house! Grandpa Joe said they could roast marshmallows, and he would tell them a monster story. Jonah thought this was a great idea.

But all that week, Harold and Louise kept taking Jonah's things! They found the new book his dad had given him and got yoghurt all over it. Then, they ate the last two pieces of chocolate cake before Jonah could have any!

The night of the campout, Harold and Louise were very excited, but Jonah was madder than ever. After dinner, Grandpa Joe and the kids took the camping supplies outside.

While Grandpa Joe started the fire, Jonah put up the big tent. Louise and Harold went looking for sticks long enough to roast their marshmallows.

When he had put up the tent, Jonah sat next to Grandpa Joe by the fire and asked to hear the monster story. Grandpa Joe waited until the twins were back before he started.

"This is a story about the Gribble. The Gribble is taller than our house and covered in grey fur. He has giant red eyes and ears on his feet.

He hunts by flipping across the forest. He looks while on his feet and listens when balancing on his hands. When he hears a kid who won't share toys or takes things without asking, he follows them home to gobble them up!

Harold and Louise looked very scared. They shivered while looking at Grandpa Joe with wide eyes. Jonah had to admit he was a little scared too. He wrapped himself in a blanket.

Harold and Louise moved closer to him and tried to get under his blanket. It was too small for all three of them, so Jonah grabbed it back and told them to get their own. The twins ran into the tent and hid.

Grandpa Joe said it was bedtime anyway, so Jonah should get into his sleeping bag while he would put out the fire. Jonah went into the tent, ignoring the twins. He got into his sleeping bag and fell asleep.

Jonah woke up when he felt hands shaking him. It was Louise! Jonah looked around the tent and saw that Harold was staring outside the tent flap.

Louise whispered in his ear. They had seen the Gribble, and it was getting closer. Jonah went out and looked outside the tent. At first, he couldn't see anything, just the shape of the house in the moonlight.

But then, he saw glowing eyes. They were huge, looking over the top of the house. Jonah grabbed Harold and pulled him back into the tent, zipping up the flap.

Jonah felt a pit in his stomach. He felt like it was his fault that the Gribble had come for them. He told the twins he was sorry for not sharing his toys. Harold and Louise shook their heads. They were sorry too! They should have asked to share instead of taking.

Jonah and the twins hugged each other tightly. Jonah handed them the blanket he had been wearing when they were in front of the fire. He told them to get under it and hide. Jonah would run to the house and wake up dad and Cindy. The twins were scared, but they gave him a big hug and went to hide.

Jonah looked outside to see where the Gribble was hiding, but couldn't see it anywhere. Jonah grabbed his flashlight, took a deep breath, and stepped outside.

He ran right into a solid shape! It must be the Gribble! He closed his eyes as tight as he could and waited for the monster to gobble him right up.

But nothing happened. Jonah opened his eyes to see Grandpa Joe with a confused expression. Jonah told him they had to get help. The Gribble was hiding behind the house!

Grandpa Joe looked around and told Joe to tell him exactly what happened. Jonah told him about the red eyes and told the twins to hide under the blanket. When he was done, Grandpa Joe gave him a big smile and told Jonah to come back into the tent with him.

Safely back in the tent, Grandpa Joe told Jonah and the twins that they got rid of the Gribble on their own. Harold asked how, and Grandpa Joe said that the Gribble only wants to eat selfish children.

Jonah said it was surely because they had apologised and shared the blanket. Grandpa Joe said that was good, but only sharing the most important thing you can give would get rid of him.

Louise asked what that was, and Grandpa Joe smiled and told them it was love. They took care of each other when the Gribble came and scared off the biggest monster in the woods!

Jonah and the twins smiled at each other. The twins lifted the blanket, and they all squeezed in it together and fell asleep.

The New Thief in School

Ron loved going to school. His school was small and not many children attended, but it was lots of fun. It was by a river in the woods and the class would play games, read stories, and go for walks with their teacher, Miss Maple.

Every morning, the students would queue by Miss Maple's desk and she would give each child an orange from a basket. The oranges were from her very own orange tree. They were delicious and made the classroom smell wonderful. Everyone loved Miss Maple's oranges, but Ron especially!

On a sunny spring day, a new boy arrived at school. Miss Maple brought him to the front of the class and introduced him as Elliot. Elliot gave a big smile and said hello. He said he was happy to meet everyone and looked forward to playing together.

Ron wasn't sure if he was happy to meet Elliot. Ron had gone to school with his friends since they were little. They all knew each other, but no one knew Elliot.

When Elliot sat down, some of the other students began to whisper. They whispered about how Elliot's clothes were different from their clothes, and how Elliot spoke differently than the way they spoke. Once Elliot heard the whispering, he didn't say another word for the rest of the day.

The next day, Ron came to class and waited in line by Miss Maple's desk to say good morning and have an orange from the basket. But the basket was empty!

Ron's classmates began to whisper. The oranges had never been stolen before. Elliot was new in class, which meant that Elliot must have stolen the oranges! Ron didn't whisper but he nodded his head in agreement.

When he came to class, Elliot could hear everyone whispering about him again. He went to his desk and sat down. All morning, the children played and had fun. Elliot just sat by himself and said nothing.

At lunchtime, Miss Maple asked Ron why no one was playing with Elliot. Ron said they thought he looked different and spoke strangely. They also believed he had stolen the oranges.

Miss Maple asked Ron if he remembered his first day at school. Ron thought hard but couldn't remember much. Miss Maple said that on Ron's first day, he was a stranger. The other kids had played with each other their entire lives, but Ron was new in town.

Now Ron remembered. He had wanted to play with his classmates but didn't know how to join in. He had felt lonely and sad.

Miss Maple asked Ron if he thought Elliot might feel the same way. Ron nodded. He thought about how hurtful it is to have people whisper mean or untrue things about you.

Ron stood up and walked up to Elliot's desk. He smiled and introduced himself. Ron told Elliot about how the oranges had been stolen. Elliot looked shocked. He loved oranges and felt terrible that no one got their morning treat. Ron said if Elliot wanted to help, he had a plan to catch the thief!

Ron said they should come to school early and hide under the desk to await the return of the thief. They could solve the mystery together! Elliot gave Ron a big smile. He was in!

Ron and Elliot told Miss Maple their plan and asked if she could bring more oranges to lure the thief. Miss Maple said if they had permission from home, they could all come early and she would bring the oranges. Ron and Elliot got permission and went to bed happy and excited.

The next morning, Ron and Elliot came to school an hour early. Miss Maple had filled the basket with fresh oranges and waited in the lunchroom while Ron and Elliot hid.

The creature was brown with white fur on its belly. As the boys watched, it devoured an orange. When the creature was done, it cleaned its paws. Then, it took the other oranges out of the room through a tiny crack in the window, one at a time.

The boys snuck outside and quietly followed the animal to a hollow tree trunk next to the river. Ron and Elliot looked at each other in surprise.

Rushing back to the school, they told Miss Maple what they had seen and brought her back to the hollow tree trunk. The three watched and laughed as oranges fell out of the tree trunk. It was too full of oranges!

Miss Maple said the animal was a pine marten. They went back to class. Miss Maple showed them a picture book about animals that had a chapter about pine martens.

When the other students arrived, they saw the empty basket and began to whisper about Elliot again. Instead of nodding along, Ron stood with Elliot at the front of the class.

Ron said that he and Elliot had found out who the thief was. Elliot held up the picture book and showed them the photo of the pine marten. He explained how pine martens ate all kinds of food and slept during the day. That's why no one had seen one before!

Ron told about how the pine marten snuck in through a window that had been left open to let in the warm spring air. Elliot and Ron's classmates cheered. They were heroes!

Miss Maple said that she would be sure to close the window from now on. Elliot asked if she could do something else, too.

Elliot asked if Miss Maple would bring an extra orange for the pine marten next week. The whole class could come early and sit by the river. If they were quiet enough, maybe they could all see the pine marten!

The next week, Miss Maple brought an extra orange, and Ron and Elliot brought the class to the hollow log.

When the pine marten popped their fuzzy little head out of the log, the children began to whisper again. They loved the pine marten! They were so happy Elliot joined their class!

When they returned to their classroom, Ron explained to everyone what he had learned about whispering and thinking bad things about kids they didn't know. Everyone felt bad about accidentally being mean and apologised to Elliot. Elliot and Ron smiled at each other.

Now everyone in the class played together and no one whispered mean things. Ron and Elliot became especially good friends, playing by the river and learning about all the animals that lived nearby.

The Trickster's Riddle

Once there were two very different brothers. The older brother was called Liam. He was strong but impatient. The younger brother was called Riley. Riley was patient but small.

Liam walked as fast as he could, always in a hurry to get to where he was going. Riley always fell behind and had to rush to keep up with Liam, even though Riley wanted to take his time.

One day while they were walking home through the woods, Liam had gotten so far ahead that Riley couldn't see him anymore.

Riley called out to Liam, asking him to slow down. When he didn't hear any response, Riley began to run.

Riley watched his feet as he ran, careful not to trip over a stone or branch. But instead of tripping, he ran right into Liam's back and fell!

When Riley looked up from where he had fallen, he saw Liam staring at a small creature sitting on a big stone. It was furry, had pointy ears, and a great long tail.

The creature spoke to them. It said it was a pooka, a magical creature capable of granting wishes. But to earn a wish, they had to answer three riddles.

Riley asked what would happen if they got the answers wrong. The pooka warned that if they got the riddles wrong, they would have to give the pooka their most valuable thing.

Riley told Liam that they should just go home. He knew that pookas were tricksters who never played fair! But Liam ignored his brother and said he could easily answer all the riddles. The pooka smiled.

For the first riddle, the pooka asked what Liam could add to a barrel that would make it lighter.

Liam didn't hesitate before he replied that it was air. If you put air in a barrel, it would make it lighter. The pooka smiled.

For the second riddle, the pooka asked where Liam could find gold where no real gold could be found.

Liam laughed. A gold mine, of course! The gold was in the mine, but you couldn't see it until you dug it out! The pooka's smile grew even bigger.

For the third riddle, the pooka asked which rock was as light as a blade of grass. Liam grinned. He said he knew this was a trick question.

There was no such thing as a rock as light as a blade of grass! The pooka gave a mean grin, showing two rows of big pointy teeth.

A yellow glow shone in its eyes. Suddenly, Liam vanished! Riley asked what the pooka had done with his brother.

The pooka said he had only done as he had promised. Liam got all the answers wrong, so he had taken Liam's most precious thing: his freedom.

The pooka laughed and asked if Riley wanted to try to answer the riddles too. Riley thought for a moment.

The pooka's ears twitched impatiently and he asked again if Riley wanted to try to earn a wish.

After he thought for a long time, Riley answered yes. The pooka gave another big smile.

The pooka repeated the first riddle, asking what Riley could add to a barrel that would make it lighter.

Riley thought for a long time. Then, he asked the pooka to repeat the question. The pooka rolled its eyes but repeated the riddle.

After several minutes, Riley said that if you add a hole to a barrel, that would make the barrel lighter.

If the barrel was full, the hole would let what was inside out. If the barrel was empty, a hole would be like cutting off a piece of the barrel, which would also make it lighter.

The pooka snarled and said that Riley had just made a lucky guess.

The pooka said Riley would never get the second one! Then the pooka repeated the second riddle, asking Riley where there was gold in a place where no real gold could be found.

Riley repeated the riddle to himself and tapped his chin with his finger. The pooka grew impatient and demanded that Riley answer.

Riley said that the pooka never said how quickly he had to answer, so he was going to take his time. The pooka's fur bristled. It was very angry, but Riley kept calm.

Finally, Riley gave his answer. He told the pooka you couldn't get real gold from the dictionary, but you could find the word gold.

The pooka grew even angrier. It stomped its feet and shook its fists. Riley waited patiently for the pooka to finish his temper tantrum.

When it was done, the pooka repeated the final riddle through clenched teeth. What kind of rock was as light as a blade of grass?

Riley thought longer than he had for any of the other riddles. The pooka huffed and puffed, furious at

Riley for making him wait. Riley stayed calm, refusing to be rushed. Then the answer came to him.

Smiling, Riley said that a shamrock was as light as a blade of grass. It wasn't a real rock, but it had the word rock in it, so it still counted!

The pooka was angrier than anyone had ever been in the entire world! It had never been bested before! Now it would have to grant this puny human boy any wish he wanted!

Riley waited for the pooka to stop stomping and screaming. When it fell silent, Riley made his wish.

He wished for his brother's freedom! The pooka howled with rage and disappeared. Then Liam appeared holding an axe in his hand. Riley asked if he was alright. Liam said he was so tired!

The pooka had told Liam that he had to chop an endless pile of firewood. No matter how quickly Liam chopped, the pile never grew smaller.

Liam said he tried to chop as much as possible, but the pile of wood was always the same. He eventually understood he had to slow down because rushing wouldn't make the job easier.

Liam asked Riley how he had freed him. Riley said he had answered the riddles and wished for Liam's freedom. Liam was astounded!

How had Riley been able to do what his bigger and faster brother wasn't able to? Riley said that he had listened to the riddles carefully and taken his time.

Liam was very impressed. From that day on, Liam made sure to always walk with Riley, never ahead. For the first time in his life, Liam didn't rush and paid attention.

Riley and the pooka's riddles taught him that rushing could lead to mistakes, and paying attention could be worth its weight in gold.

Not-So-Super Tony's Tall Tales

Tony was a regular boy who went to a regular school. Most of his classmates were also regular, but some of them were superheroes!

Tony's friend Jemma could fly. Once, Jemma rescued a kitten stuck in a tree and got a ball back when it had accidentally been kicked onto the roof. On the same day! Everyone loved Jemma.

Tony's friend Franklin could move things with his mind! Franklin had used his powers to stop a little kid from walking into the street, and everyone cheered.

Tony's friend Charlie could walk through anything he wanted! Last year, when a fire had started in the science room, the teacher couldn't get the closet door open to get the fire extinguisher. Charlie had walked through the door and put out the fire! Charlie had been given a special prize by the school for being brave.

Tony loved his friends, but he couldn't help but feel completely un-special compared to them. And this made him feel bad about himself.

One day, while sitting in the lunchroom, Tony was thinking about how unimportant he was. Tony must have looked very sad because Franklin asked Tony what was wrong. Tony didn't want to explain, so he mumbled something about not having powers. Franklin's eyes brightened and he congratulated

Tony. Tony was confused. What did Franklin think he had done?

For the rest of the day, everyone was paying attention to Tony. People gave him high-fives and told him how cool he was. At snack time, Tony got the biggest piece of banana bread. During afternoon break, he got to play any game he wanted and didn't even have to wait his turn.

When they were walking home from school, Tony asked Jemma if she had noticed people treating him differently. Jemma smiled and said it was because everyone was so excited about Tony's new powers!

Tony's eyes widened in surprise. Why did people think he had powers? Tony thought back to lunchtime, Franklin had congratulated him. Franklin must have misheard what Tony said. Now everyone thought Tony had powers!

That night while he was waiting to fall asleep, Tony thought about what a great day he had. If this was what it was like to be a superhero, maybe he could lie going a little longer. What would it hurt?

For the rest of the week, Tony felt like a superstar. Everyone paid attention to him, let him jump to the front of the queue, and gave him the best parts of their lunch. Tony didn't even have to ask! People just kept being extra nice to him.

But by the next week, people seemed irritated. They started asking Tony when he was going to show them his new powers. Finally, one of the older kids said that Tony had to show them after school, or else. Tony felt trapped. What was he going to do?

When the final bell of the day rang, everyone was waiting for Tony by the swings. He felt sick to his stomach. What was he going to say? As Tony walked up to the big group of kids, he had an idea.

Tony slipped his water bottle into the sleeve of his jacket, careful not to let anyone see him do it. When he got to the swings, he nervously told the crowd that his new power was controlling water. Tony popped the cap off of the water bottle and splashed the water in the air.

Tony had hoped that it would make a big wave, but all it did was splash on his head. Everyone laughed at him! The older kids called him a liar and soon, Tony was wet and alone. He sat on one of the swings, feeling so ashamed he could cry.

Then he heard someone say hello. Tony looked up. Standing in front of him were Franklin, Jemma, and Charlie. Tony expected them to be mad, but they looked worried. Charlie asked if Tony was okay.

Tony didn't know what to say at first. Then, he decided that the best answer was the truth. Tony said that he felt terrible. He said that he was ashamed of lying and sorry that he hadn't been a better friend.

Franklin said that it was okay, they just wanted to know why Tony had lied.

Tony said that he should have corrected Franklin when he misunderstood him but when people thought he was a superhero, they treated him like he was important.

Tony told them how un-special he had felt compared to his super friends. They were all so incredible, and Tony was just a nobody.

Tony said he understood if Jemma, Charlie, and Franklin didn't want to be friends anymore.

Now, Tony's friends were surprised. Why would they not want to be friends anymore? Jemma sat on the swing next to him and said that even though Tony didn't feel special, they all thought he was super. Tony asked Jemma what she meant.

Jemma said that she may have gotten the kitten down from the tree with her powers, but Tony had knocked on every door in town until he found the kitten's home and reunited her with her family. Tony was so smart and tenacious, he could still be a hero.

Charlie asked if Tony remembered when she was failing maths. She reminded Tony that he worked with her for a whole month to help her pass the big test. Tony even missed a trip to the amusement park to help her!

Franklin told Tony that he was always saving people. Franklin said that he was so forgetful that he often forgot his lunch. But Tony always shared his with Franklin, or with anyone else who didn't have enough to eat. That was pretty super to him, Franklin said

Tony didn't know what to say. He still felt like crying, but now it was because he was so happy. He thanked Franklin, Jemma, and Charlie. Tony said it didn't matter to him anymore if he had powers. He had the best friends who made him feel like the most super person on the planet.

The four friends hugged and walked home together. After that day, Tony remembered that as long as he tried his best to be a good person and appreciate the people he loved, he'd never need to lie again.

The Big Skip

Jacob always felt there was never enough time to do the fun things he liked. There always seemed to be plenty of time to do homework, the dishes, or help take care of his little brother, but when it came to video games, drawing comics, or playing with his friends, Jacob always had to leave before he was done. He was always rushing home to do something boring.

Today, Jacob was rushing home to clean his room. He had been at the park with his friend Tyler when his mom called him home. To Jacob, it felt like he had only been playing for a few minutes, but his mom said he had been gone for two whole hours! Even though Jacob wanted to keep playing, he knew it was time to go home.

Jacob ran down the street to his apartment as fast as he could. Jacob knew his mom didn't like it when he took the shortcut through the woods, but if he didn't, he would be late!

As Jacob ran into the woods, he heard a voice shouting somewhere above his head. Someone was calling for help!

But Jacob was in too much of a hurry! He shouted that he couldn't stop because he was late. The voice told Jacob that if he helped, he would give Jacob something to make sure Jacob would never be late for anything ever again.

Jacob was confused but knew he should stop anyway. It was the right thing to do! Jacob climbed up as high as he could into the tree and almost fell out when he saw a little spaceship!

It was silver, the size of a football, and badly stuck in the tree's branches. Jacob's mouth fell open in surprise. It was an alien!

Climbing the tree as quickly as he could, Jacob arrived at where the spaceship was stuck and pulled it from between two leafy branches. As soon as the spaceship came unstuck, it hovered in the air.

A little glass dome on the top of the spaceship popped open, and a little blue face popped out. The alien thanked Jacob and handed him a silver box the size of Jacob's palm. It had three buttons on it. The button at the top was blue, the one in the middle was red, and the one at the bottom was green.

The alien explained that if Jacob pressed the blue button on the box, it would skip through any activity. If Jacob pressed the red button, time would pause. If Jacob pressed the green button, time would rewind.

Jacob thanked the alien. Jacob couldn't wait to try his new gift and pressed the red button to pause time. Now that he had paused time, Jacob didn't have to rush home!

Jacob took his time, stopping to look at all the cool plants and bugs he saw along the way. When Jacob got to his front door, he pressed the red button and unpaused time.

Jacob's mom gave him a big smile when he walked in. She was so happy that Jacob was home on time. Jacob was happy too! With his new device, he didn't even have to rush!

Jacob went up to his room. He looked at the big mess and Jacob pressed the blue button. In what felt like a single second, Jacob's room was clean!

Jacob looked at his clock and saw that it was dinner time. It was his night to pick, and Jacob knew they would be having tacos! But when Jacob sat down at the table, he saw that his mom had made boiled potatoes and plain chicken.

Jacob asked why they weren't having tacos. Jacob's mom said she had asked Jacob what he wanted to eat for dinner while he was cleaning his room. Jacob hadn't answered, so instead, Jacob's little brother Tim picked.

While they ate, Jacob asked Tim if he wanted to listen to their favourite podcast together while Jacob did the dishes.

Tim said they had already listened to it together while he and Jacob had cleaned his room. Jacob was so confused! He didn't remember listening to the podcast, or Tim helping him clean!

Jacob thought that was very nice of Tim, but didn't say anything. Jacob didn't want to accidentally let slip that he didn't remember anything because of the device!

After dinner, when it was time for Jacob to do the dishes. Jacob smiled. He knew his gift would help him fast-forward through the boring clean-up.

Jacob took the dishes to the sink, put on his dishwashing gloves, and hit the blue button. In the blink of an eye, he was in the living room.

Jacob and his mom were sitting on the couch. The end of Jacob's favourite cartoon was on the TV.

Tim walked into the room and sat down next to him on the couch. Jacob's mom asked him if Jacob was going to thank Tim for helping him with the dishes.

But just like before, Jacob couldn't remember anything! He nodded and said thank you to Tim. Jacob thought very hard.

Jacob realised that during all the boring times that he had fast-forwarded, they hadn't just been doing boring things! He had also been having fun times with Tim.

Jacob pressed the green button and the device rewound time. Jacob found himself standing by the shortcut. Time skipped back to just after he had left the park to come home!

Jacob raced to where the alien was stuck. Like he had done the first time, Jacob climbed the tree and helped the alien get his ship unstuck.

This time, when the alien tried to reward him with the silver box, Jacob showed him that he already had one.

Jacob explained to the alien that this was the second time he had helped get the ship unstuck! The alien shook his little blue head. Playing with time was so confusing!

Jacob said that though he was thankful for the gift, he didn't want it anymore.

Jacob told him he knew it could be useful, but it wasn't possible to skip the things you didn't want to do. Even the boring times still had good parts

The little blue person seemed to understand. He took the device from Jacob, smiled and zipped away into the sky.

After that, Jacob went home. He was late, and his mom was cross, but he and Tim cleaned his room together while listening to their favourite podcast. It was lots of fun!

This time, when Jacob's mom asked what he wanted for dinner, Jacob immediately said tacos. After dinner, Jacob and Tim washed the dishes together. When they were done, they watched a cartoon with their mom.

From that day on, Jacob tried not to rush through the boring things so much. Some days it was harder than others. The best thing to do was to try and enjoy every moment, especially when you were with the people you loved the most!

Monster in Disguise

Ethan lived in a small village on the side of a mountain. Every day he had to walk a steep and rocky path to and from school. Ethan's classmates thought he was the bravest kid in school because the path was so dark and spooky!

One day, Ethan's entire school met in the lunchroom for a big announcement. The headmaster told them there was a monster loose on the mountain. The kids became scared and started asking questions. A monster? What kind of monster? What were they going to do?

The headmaster said the kids didn't need to be scared. This wasn't a normal monster, but one that fed on bad deeds. To eat, the monster tricked kids into doing bad things. Every time a child did a bad thing, the monster would grow stronger.

One boy asked what kind of bad deeds the monster tricked kids into doing. The teacher said that a boy down the mountain had been tricked into breaking his mom's favourite vase into a thousand pieces. Another girl had been tricked into pushing her little sister's bicycle into the lake!

Ethan's classmates seemed scared, but Ethan thought he was too brave and clever for any monster. If the monster tried to trick Ethan into breaking something or throwing something away, Ethan would just ignore it.

The headmaster said that because every adult, even the teachers, would be looking for the monster, all the children had to go home. None of the kids would be allowed to go alone. They would have to walk home in pairs. That way, they would be safe if the monster found them.

Ethan told the teachers that he didn't need a partner. He was too brave and clever for the monster. Because Ethan's classmates thought he was the bravest and didn't want to walk the spooky path with him, no one said a word. They all thought Ethan would be fine. After all, he was the bravest kid in class.

Ethan grabbed his things and began the long walk home. Ethan was so excited to have a full day to play at home! Maybe his grandma could come over and they could bake cookies together!

As he began walking the spooky and steep path up the mountain to his house, Ethan heard a noise ahead of him. He called out and asked who was there. He said that if it was the monster, the monster better run! He was way too clever to fall for any monster tricks! At first, no one answered. Then, from up the path came his grandma!

Ethan smiled, ran up to her, and gave her a great big hug. Grandma asked what he was doing out of school and Ethan explained about the monster. Grandma said they should go home where it was safe.

She said they would bake cookies and play Ethan's favourite games!

When they got home, Grandma went into the kitchen. Oh dear, Ethan heard her say. Ethan asked what was wrong. Grandma said that the eggs had gone bad. She said that if Ethan loved her, he would take the eggs outside and throw them in the rubbish bin.

Ethan was confused. His mum and dad had bought the eggs yesterday, they were fresh. But Ethan loved his Grandma, so he took the eggs outside and threw them in the big rubbish bin.

When he came back, Grandma looked sad. Oh dear, she said. Ethan asked what was wrong. Grandma said that the big mixing bowl was cracked, so Ethan had to go outside and throw it in the rubbish bin.

Ethan took the bowl and looked it over. The bowl didn't look cracked. Ethan asked Grandma if maybe she had made a mistake. Grandma said she hadn't made a mistake, and if Ethan loved her, he would do as she asked.

Ethan loved his Grandma, so he threw the bowl in the rubbish bin. He heard it crack into a hundred pieces. Throwing away the bowl made him sad because he knew it was his dad's favourite.

When Ethan came back inside, he saw that Grandma was standing in the living room. She had made a big fire in the fireplace. It was warm and smelled good. For some reason, Grandma was standing in front of the fire holding the big quilt that she had made for Ethan's birthday. She looked very sad.

When Ethan asked Grandma what was wrong, Grandma said she had gotten a chocolate stain on the quilt, and he needed to burn it in the fireplace. Ethan was confused. He couldn't see a single stain on the quilt. Even if there was, why should they burn it when they could just wash it?

Grandma told Ethan that they couldn't wash the stain out or fix the quilt. If Ethan loved her, he would do as she asked. She said she would make Ethan a new one anyway.

Ethan took the quilt in his hands and looked at every part of it, trying to find a stain. No matter how hard he looked, Ethan couldn't see a thing wrong with the quilt. He didn't want to burn the blanket, but what if Grandma thought that meant he didn't love her?

Grandma asked Ethan to throw the blanket in the fire, again. Ethan said that his parents told him to only burn wood in the fireplace. Grandma looked so sad when Ethan told her that.

Grandma asked for a third time, telling Ethan that if he loved her, he would burn the blanket. Grandma pushed Ethan closer to the fireplace. Ethan felt a knot in his tummy. He wanted to say no but felt like he couldn't.

Suddenly, the front door to the house flew open. Ethan's mom, dad, and grandma were there!

Ethan turned to look at the grandma standing next to him.

The grandma standing next to Ethan tried to sneak past his parents, but they grabbed her and took her outside. The new grandma ran up to Ethan and wrapped her arms around him.

Grandma explained that the school had called all the families to warn them about the monster. But the school had forgotten to tell the children the most important thing: to make kids do bad things, the monster disguised itself as a trusted adult. Not only had the school forgotten to warn the children, but they had also let Ethan walk home alone! His family had rushed home as fast as they could to make sure Ethan was safe.

Ethan was so upset by everything that had happened that day that he cried. He told Grandma about how he had thrown away the eggs and the bowl. Grandma hugged him tight and said it didn't matter. It was very brave of Ethan to hold onto the quilt. But Ethan didn't feel very brave at all anymore.

When Ethan's parents came back inside, they said that the monster couldn't trick anyone ever again. They had painted the monster from head to toe in green with paint that could never wash off. That way, no matter what shape the monster took, it could never trick anyone again!

That night, Ethan and Grandma baked cookies and talked. Ethan told Grandma that he had thought he was too brave for the monster to trick. Grandma said that Ethan had been braver than he had been in his entire life! The bravest thing in the world was to do the right thing, even when people you love say it's wrong.

Grandma told Ethan a trick he could use if he ever got confused again, by a monster or anyone else. Grandma said that people who really loved him would never ask Ethan to do anything that made him sad. Ethan hugged Grandma tight.

After Grandma tucked him in, Ethan went to sleep feeling safe and loved. Ethan knew that even though the monster had scared him, it had taught him the true meaning of bravery.

Hakeem Gets What He Deserves

Hakeem and Omar were brothers who were very different from each other.

Omar was the younger brother. Omar loved to play the piano, but he had very short fingers. Because Omar couldn't reach all the keys, his songs never sounded quite right.

Omar loved to play football, too. As much as he loved football, Omar was quite clumsy on the pitch. Sometimes, he even tripped over his own feet! Omar's favourite subject in school was English. But as much as he loved to read, he never got very good grades.

Hakeem was the older brother. Hakeem was graceful and loved to play the violin. Hakeem was good at sports and school, too. Everyone praised Hakeem and told him how nice and talented he was.

But Omar knew the truth about his brother. Hakeem was a mean bully!

Hakeem would always take the remote control from Omar when they were watching TV and make them watch boring animal documentaries. When Omar tried to play a new song on the piano for their parents, Hakeem would pick up his violin and play along so loudly that no one could hear Omar's playing!

Hakeem even got Omar in trouble about his grades. Once, Omar had tried to hide a bad grade he had gotten on a book report. But Hakeem had found it and showed it to their parents at dinner! They got mad at Omar, but Hakeem didn't get in any trouble for being a tattle-tale or going through Omar's things!

Omar grew so angry at Hakeem's bullying, that he came up with a plan to get revenge. Hakeem had a big violin recital coming up, so before he went to perform in front of all their friends and family, Omar would put a stink bug in his violin!

When Hakeem started to play his violin, the stink bug would get angry and make a terrible smell. Hakeem would have to stop playing and everyone would think he was a violinist who was as bad at playing as he smelled!

The week before the recital, Omar found the biggest, smelliest stink bug in his entire garden. He put it in a jar he had found, poking holes in the lid and making sure to add some leaves so the bug had something to eat.

That week, Omar didn't get mad at Hakeem once. When Hakeem changed the channel and made them watch a show about bears, Omar said nothing. When

Hakeem played over Omar's piano song, Omar said nothing. When Hakeem asked Omar if he wanted help with his English homework, Omar just smiled.

On the day of the recital, Omar was so excited. He waited until Hakeem was busy eating breakfast, grabbed the jar with the stink bug, and snuck up to Hakeem's bedroom.

Once he was inside Hakeem's room, Omar closed the door quietly. He crept over to the violin case and began to open the lid on the jar. He froze when he heard someone opening the door. Turning slowly, Omar saw it was Hakeem!

Hakeem stood in the doorway of his bedroom looking very surprised. He asked what Omar was doing. Omar was so mad that Hakeem had spoiled his plan to get revenge!

Omar stomped his foot and yelled at Hakeem about all the mean things he had done to him. Omar said that everyone thought Hakeem was perfect but Omar knew he was a bully who just wanted all the attention.

After Omar was done yelling at him, Hakeem looked even more surprised. Hakeem sat down on his bed and looked very sad. Hakeem said he had no idea he had been making Omar feel so badly. Omar said he didn't believe Hakeem for one second!

Hakeem said he was telling the truth. When he changed the channels to nature documentaries, it was because he remembered how much Omar had loved animals when they were little. Omar thought for a minute and remembered this was true. He had loved watching animal documentaries.

Hakeem said that when Omar played the piano, he wanted to play with him, not over him. Hakeem was so proud of Omar's piano playing. Omar was surprised. He didn't know that his brother wanted to play music with him.

Hakeem explained that he had told their parents about Omar's grade not because he wanted to get him in trouble or embarrass him, but because Hakeem used to get in trouble all the time for lying about his grades. This part really surprised Omar, who had always thought that Hakeem did well at school.

Hakeem said that he used to struggle in English class just like Omar did. Their parents were mad when they found out Hakeem had been lying, but then they had gotten a tutor for Hakeem and that had really helped.

Now Omar didn't feel angry at all. He felt really bad. Omar had thought that Hakeem was the biggest jerk on the planet. The truth was, the two brothers just didn't know each other very well. Omar felt guilty about the prank.

Hakeem said he was sorry for everything. He loved Omar and was trying to be a good big brother. Hakeem said that if he wanted to, Omar could still play the prank, and he would pretend he didn't know. Hakeem deserved to get sprayed by a stink bug during the rehearsal for everything he had done.

This made Omar even sadder. Hakeem must have felt very bad about how he had treated him! Omar thought long and hard. Then he took the jar with the stink bug, opened the window, and let it out.

Hakeem smiled and asked Omar if he would forgive him for being mean. Omar said yes, but only if Hakeem forgave Omar for thinking so many bad things about him.

From that day on, whenever Omar felt upset about something that Hakeem did, Omar would talk about his feelings instead of being angry and silent. Talking about his feelings was hard, but it always made things better.

And now, whenever Omar heard Hakeem playing the violin, Omar would join him, playing along on the piano. Over time, they learned to play together beautifully, neither one playing louder than the other.

Chocolate and Orange

Chocolate was a little brown goat who lived on a beautiful farm. He was sweet and friendly and loved to play with everyone. Except for Orange.

Orange was an old barn cat. Once, Chocolate asked Orange to go jumping on hay bales and running around on the grass. Orange turned up his nose at the little goat and told him he didn't play silly games like that.

Orange told Chocolate that he was very busy keeping pests like mice and rats out of the barn. If too many mice and rats got in, they would eat the entire harvest, so Orange's job was very important.

This had hurt Chocolate's feelings. As far as Chocolate could tell, Orange didn't work that much and mostly napped. From then on, Chocolate didn't pay any attention to Orange. Orange was boring anyway. Chocolate couldn't butt heads, he didn't have hooves and took too many naps.

One day, Chocolate was jumping around in the first rain of the summer. He was having so much fun until he saw Orange running out of the barn.

Orange was chasing a big rat that had been eating grain in the barn. Chocolate had never seen an animal run as fast as Orange, not even the horses! Chocolate was very impressed.

When he was running after the rat, Orange saw Chocolate jumping in the mud. He was impressed by how high Chocolate could jump. Chocolate could jump even higher than the rabbits!

But the two ignored each other. Chocolate went back to jumping in his puddle and Orange kept chasing the rat.

Chocolate was having the best time. The rain had made it so muddy outside and he was making such big splashes! But soon, he saw it was getting dark outside and he decided to go back into the barn.

Orange came back after chasing the rat away. He had shown that rat who was boss! Now it was dinner, and Orange had to return to the barn. He walked past the big puddle and saw that Chocolate was covered in mud! Orange turned up his nose at the little goat and walked past him.

But suddenly, Orange was stuck! As it had grown darker, the mud had gotten colder. Orange was frozen in place. He couldn't move!

Chocolate couldn't help but laugh to himself. Orange thought he was so smart. We'll look at him now! Chocolate continued to walk back to the barn. But soon, Chocolate found himself having the same trouble as Orange. Uh, oh! Chocolate couldn't lift his back hoof! It was stuck in the mud!

Orange was hissing and spitting he was so angry. He looked over at Chocolate and saw that he was stuck too. Orange told Chocolate it was all his fault they were stuck. If Chocolate hadn't been jumping in the mud, it wouldn't have gotten so sticky!

Chocolate couldn't believe that Orange blamed him! If Orange had been watching where he was going instead of acting like a snob, he wouldn't have gotten stuck in the mud!

After a while, the little goat and the cat stopped struggling against the mud. They stood in silence, stuck in the mud together. But it was getting cold and they were going to miss dinnertime at the barn if they didn't get out soon!

Orange looked around them, trying to think of a solution. A-ha! Right above Chocolate's head was a big branch. Orange knew that if Chocolate could jump high enough, he could use the branch to pull himself up. Then Chocolate could go get help from someone smarter!

Orange told Chocolate that even though he couldn't jump as high as a cat, Chocolate should try to grab that branch above him with his teeth and pull himself out. Then Chocolate could get a more clever animal to help Orange.

Chocolate thought this was a very rude thing for Orange to say, but tried the plan anyway. He kicked off with his three free hooves and jumped as high as he could. Stretching his neck as far as it could go, Chocolate grabbed the branch with his teeth and yanked with all his might.

With a pop, Chocolate's hooves came unstuck from the mud and he landed on the soft grass. Orange meowed with excitement and told him to run and get help. Chocolate rolled his eyes.

Chocolate knew he was strong enough to help Orange on his own. Instead of going to get help, he walked to the edge of the big mud puddle and took the scruff of Orange's neck in his mouth.

Very gently, Chocolate pulled until Orange's little paws came unstuck from the mud. Just as gently, Chocolate placed Orange on the grass.

Orange was very surprised. He had thought this little goat was too silly to do anything so clever.

Chocolate was surprised as well. He hadn't believed that the cat could trust anyone enough to let them help him.

From that day onward, Chocolate made an effort to be more like Orange, and Orange tried to be more like Chocolate. Chocolate and Orange would take naps in the sun together. After their naps, Orange would go and jump on hay bales with Chocolate.

Even though they had very different talents, they had learned to value the best in each other. In the end, Chocolate and Orange paired very well together.

The Most Important Boy on the Moon

Caleb was the middle child in a family of super-smart super-scientists that lived on the moon. His parents studied rocks, his older brother studied space, and his older sister studied robots. Caleb didn't like science, so instead of inviting him along to do experiments, his family would make him take care of his little brother and sister. Caleb didn't mind, though. Caleb loved spending time with his family.

Because he loved spending time with his family, even though he didn't want to do science experiments, Caleb still felt left out. Like the time his big brother, big sister, and parents went out on the moon buggy to go look at rocks. Caleb didn't care about the rocks, but the moon buggy looked like so much fun! He would have loved to spend a day bouncing over rocks with his entire family.

Caleb tried to tell his parents how they felt, but they didn't listen. They were so busy doing science experiments and building robots that they never really paid attention to what Caleb and the little kids were doing.

Caleb didn't want his little brother and sister to feel sad like he did sometimes, so when they got left behind he always made sure they had a really fun time. They would build forts out of moon rocks and make moon cookies.

Caleb would tell stories he made up himself, and they would draw pictures to go with the stories. He would even help the younger kids learn important things like teaching them to tie the laces on their space boots.

After a big day of playing and learning while their parents were out in the moon buggy with his older brother and sister, Caleb's parents came home to say that they had made an incredible discovery!

They met a family of Moon People, and that family would soon be coming over for dinner! Caleb's parents and older siblings were so excited! They hadn't even known that there were other people on the moon!

Caleb was so excited to meet them, too. But his parents said that after dinner, Caleb and the little kids should stay in their room.

Caleb's parents said that the Moon People were very scientific. The Moon People had robots, and supercomputers, and built giant buildings out of moon rocks! They probably didn't want to talk with people who weren't interested in science. This made Caleb sad, but he just nodded his head.

That night, when the Moon People arrived for dinner, they were very kind and friendly, making sure to learn everyone's name and ask them about themselves. But Caleb's older siblings and parents kept trying to talk about science.

Caleb's big brother wanted to talk about space. The Moon People didn't want to talk about space. Caleb's big sister wanted to talk about robots. The Moon People didn't want to talk about robots. Caleb's parents wanted to talk about moon rocks. The Moon People didn't want to talk about moon rocks.

Soon, it became clear that all the family of Moon People wanted to do was talk to Caleb and his little brother and sister.

The Moon People asked lots of questions about what they did all day. Caleb told the Moon People about baking cookies, building forts, telling stories, and learning to tie space boot laces together.

The Moon People said they had never done any of these things. They asked Caleb and his little sister and brother if they could come over and play together one day. Caleb was very surprised but agreed. Caleb was always happy to make new friends!

Caleb's parents, older brother, and sister were confused. The Moon People knew so much about all the important kinds of science. Why would they care what little kids did all day?

The Moon People agreed that they had a lot of scientific knowledge. They had robots, knew all about space, and even built giant towers from rocks.

For as long as Moon People had existed, they spent their entire lives learning about science. Talking with Caleb, his little brother, and his little sister, they now understood that there were other important things in life to learn.

All the Moon People wanted to do now was learn as much as they could about baking, art, playing and family.

Caleb's parents and older brother and sister were shocked. But the Moon People were so smart, they must be right. Maybe they spent too much time on science and needed to learn more about how to be a family.

Caleb's parents said they were sorry to Caleb and his brothers and sisters. They had spent so much time being super scientists when they should have been putting just as much effort into being a family. Could Caleb teach them more about being a family, too? Caleb smiled and said he would be happy too.

After that night, Caleb's family spent just as much time together doing family things as they did on science experiments. Every week, the Moon People would come and have dinner with them. And now, when there were moon buggy rides, no one was left behind.

The Unchanging Castle

Oliver was a boy who loved routine. Every morning, Oliver woke up, ate breakfast, put on his favourite hat, and walked to school with his friends. When Oliver got home from school, he would do his homework, eat dinner, read a book, and go to bed.

One day, when Oliver came home from school his parents were waiting. They had big news. They were all going to move to Mars! Oliver's parents had been hired to build a new machine on Mars. When the machine was finished, people would be able to travel between Mars and Earth by stepping into a booth and pressing a button.

Oliver couldn't believe his ears! He didn't want to move to Mars! He loved his life and didn't want anything to change! Oliver thought hard about how to convince his parents to stay on Earth, but he couldn't think of anything. So Oliver decided that after dinner, he would pack a bag and run away. If Oliver's parents couldn't find him, they couldn't make him move to Mars!

After his parents thought he'd gone to be, Oliver snuck out his bedroom window, down the drainpipe, and through the backyard. He ran as fast as he could until he got to the bus stop down the street. Oliver sat on the bench and waited for the bus to come. He wasn't sure where he was going, but anywhere on Earth was better than Mars.

Oliver waited and waited, but the bus never came. Oliver was so tired that he started crying. Suddenly, Oliver heard a voice from behind him. Behind the bus stop stood a tall man with a big grey beard.

The man asked why Oliver was so sad. Oliver explained that his parents were going to make him move to Mars but he didn't want to go. The man nodded. He said that he understood exactly how Oliver felt. He didn't like change either. Oliver asked the man what he did when people tried to make him change. The man smiled.

He told Oliver that his name was the Wizard Rune. The Wizard said he hated change so much that he had built a magical castle where nothing could ever change. In the garden, it was always a sunny, summer day. Inside, the clock always stayed at four in the afternoon, and the calendar was always set to August.

Oliver was excited. His birthday was in August! The Wizard Rune asked the boy if he would like to come and live in the castle and be his apprentice. He would teach Oliver how to become a wizard!

Oliver agreed right away and he followed the Wizard Rune through the woods behind the bus stop. Just past an enchanted gate, Oliver saw the castle. Even though it was dark outside when he ran away from home, the sun shone on the castle. It was so big and beautiful!

The first thing Oliver did when he arrived at the castle was to send a magical note to his parents. He explained that he was staying on Earth and becoming a wizard. They wrote back about how sad and told him he could change his mind at any time. Oliver would always be welcome home. This made Oliver sad, but he knew he would rather live in a castle where nothing changed if it meant he could still see his friends at school.

At first, Oliver loved the castle. The Wizard Rune taught him a little bit of magic every day, and it never rained. There were little things that bugged Oliver, like how hard it was to sleep when it was always so bright outside, but he was mostly happy.

Soon, Oliver noticed bigger problems. Though Oliver could leave the castle to go to school, he could never get there on time! Inside the castle walls, clocks never changed. But time kept moving outside the castle, so no matter how hard he tried, the school was always over by the time he arrived.

As time passed outside the castle, things got worse. Though for Oliver, things never changed, Oliver's friends would come to see him and talk about the fun new things they got to do. They also started getting taller and stronger than Oliver. Even though it was always the month of August at the castle, Oliver realized it was never his birthday, so he never got any bigger or older.

One day, Oliver's friends stopped coming to visit. When Oliver asked the Wizard Rune if he had maybe changed where the entrance was, or moved the castle somewhere new, The Wizard Rune just smiled sadly. The wizard hadn't changed anything. But time outside the castle still passed, and Oliver's friends had finished school and grown-up.

In fact, so much time had passed outside the castle, some of his old classmates had even started families of their own and had children Oliver's age. Others now lived very far away. The Wizard Rune said that his parent's invention had worked. Now, many people lived on Mars.

The Wizard Rune told Oliver that because they couldn't stop things from changing outside the castle, it meant that they couldn't completely avoid the pain of change. The Wizard Rune's explanation made Oliver very sad. He hadn't thought about his parents for a long time. They must be so old now! Oliver began to cry. The Wizard Rune put a hand on his shoulder.

Oliver asked why the Wizard Rune bothered to make the castle if he couldn't stop change from happening. The wizard said it was a lesson that had taken him much longer to learn than Oliver. By the time the Wizard Rune figured out the big problem with the castle, it was too late. But luckily, it wasn't too late for Oliver!

The Wizard Rune smiled and said that he could make a new door that would allow Oliver to go back to his home on the same night he left. Oliver stopped crying and smiled. He was grateful to the wizard but wanted very much to go home. The wizard lifted his arm in the air and made complicated shapes with his fingers.

A giant wooden door appeared! Oliver asked the Wizard Rune if he could still visit him at the castle if he went through the new door. The Wizard gave the biggest smile Oliver had ever seen him make and said he would like that very much. Oliver could come back to the unchanging castle whenever he wanted.

When Oliver stepped through the door, it was evening again. He ran all the way home to his house and burst through the front door. His parents were so surprised! They hadn't even noticed that he'd left his room!

Oliver told them he had been on an adventure, and now understood that change was something you couldn't avoid. It was hard, but you needed it to grow. Oliver's parents were confused but happy that Oliver had come home.

After they moved to Mars, Oliver found that though it was different, he quite liked it. It wasn't long before his parents finished their invention, just as the Wizard Rune had told him they would. With the new machine, Oliver was able to visit his friends on Earth whenever he wanted.

Now when big changes happened, Oliver didn't worry so much about what he was losing, but about all the wonderful possibilities they could bring.

***

Disclaimer

This book contains opinions and ideas of the author and is meant to teach the reader informative and helpful knowledge while due care should be taken by the user in the application of the information provided. The instructions and strategies are possibly not right for every reader and there is no guarantee that they work for everyone. Using this book and implementing the information/ recipes therein contained is explicitly your own responsibility and risk. This work with all its contents, does not guarantee correctness, completion, quality or correctness of the provided information. Misinformation or misprints cannot be completely eliminated.

Printed in Great Britain
by Amazon